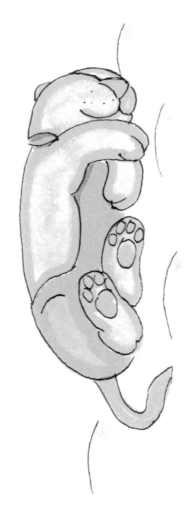

HERBERT THE LION

This edition published in 1998 by SMITHMARK Publishers, a division of
U.S. Media Holdings, Inc., 115 West 18th Street, New York, NY 10011.

SMITHMARK books are available for bulk purchase for sales promotion
and premium use. For details write or call the manager of special sales,
SMITHMARK Publishers, 115 West 18th Street, New York, NY 10011;
212-519-1300.

Library of Congress Catalog Card Number: 97-62214
ISBN: 0-7651-9057-5

Printed in Hong Kong
1 0 9 8 7 6 5 4 3 2 1

HERBERT THE LION

Story and Pictures by
CLARE TURLAY NEWBERRY

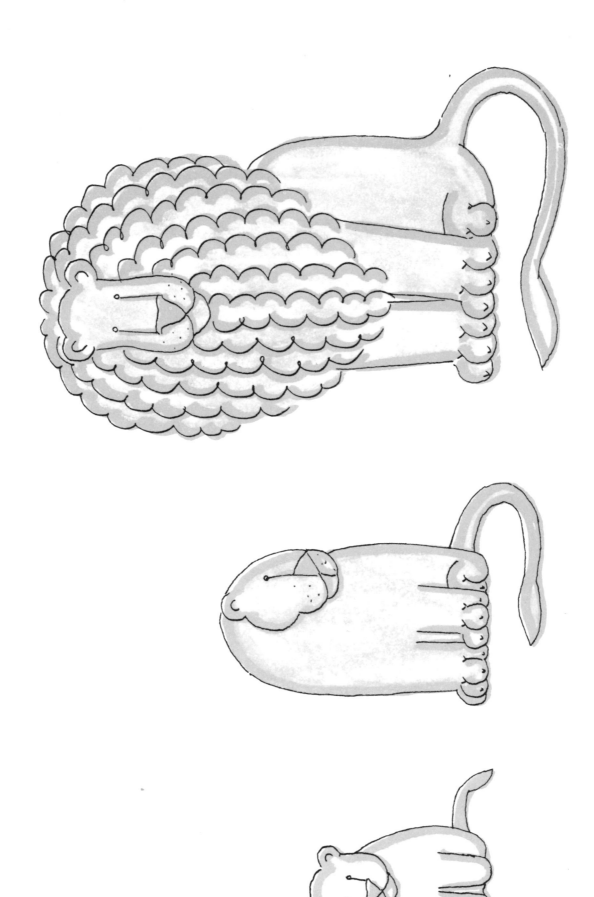

There was once a little girl named Sally
who wanted a baby lion.

She already had a doll's house, two dolls,
a tea set, and a toy zebra on wheels,
but she didn't like any of them.

All she wanted was a lion,

a real, live lion.

So one day her mother brought her one from downtown.

Then Sally was very happy.

She named the little cub Herbert,

and they played together all day long.

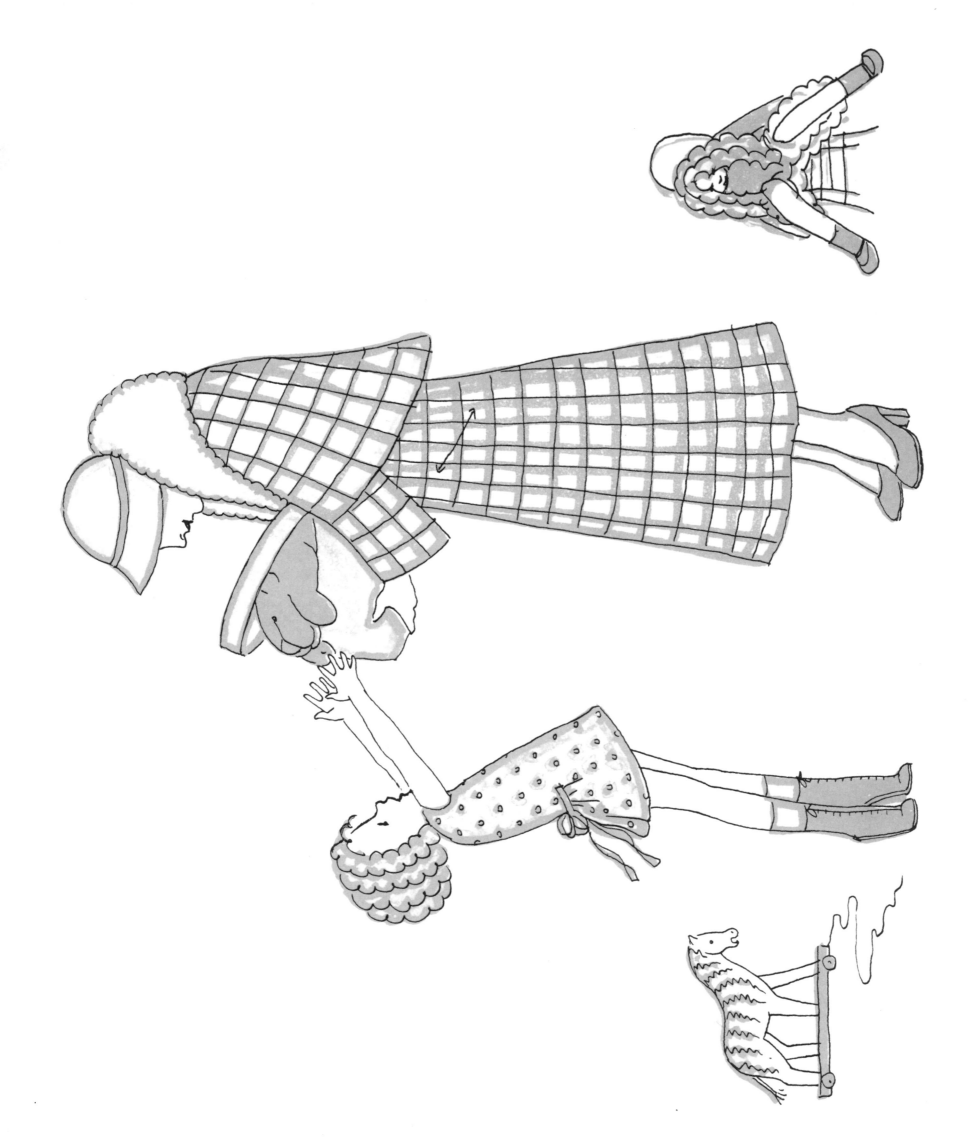

Every morning Herbert had a hot cooked cereal for breakfast.
For lunch he had spinach and poached egg.
For supper he had baked potato and applesauce
and a round cookie with raisins in it.

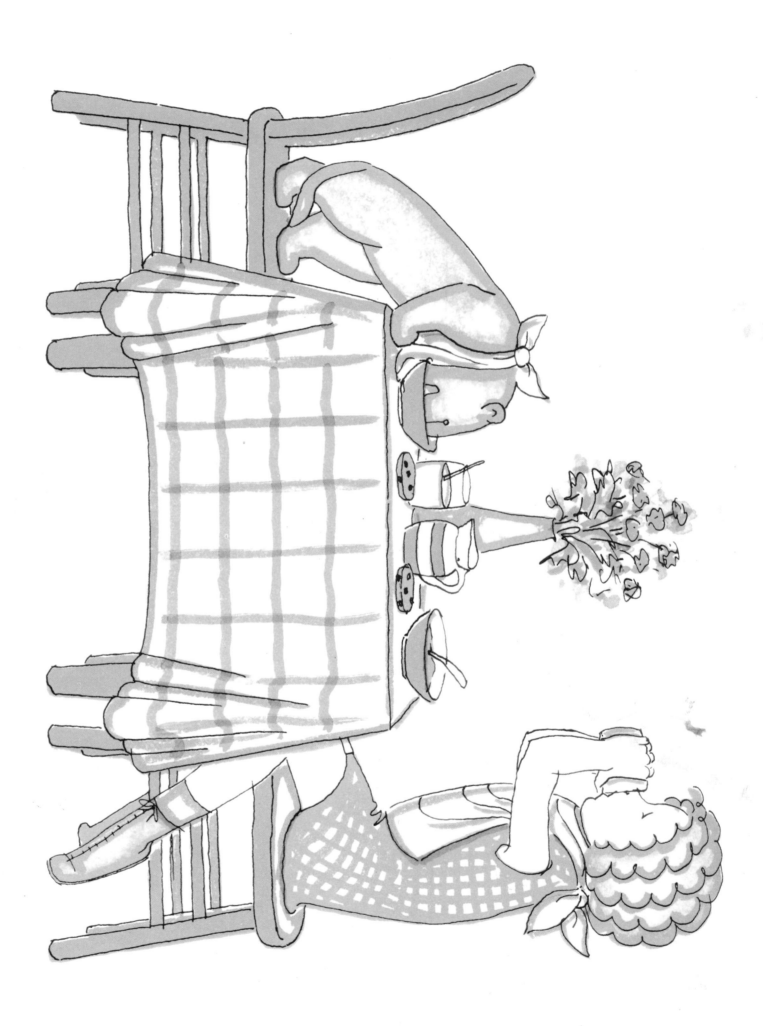

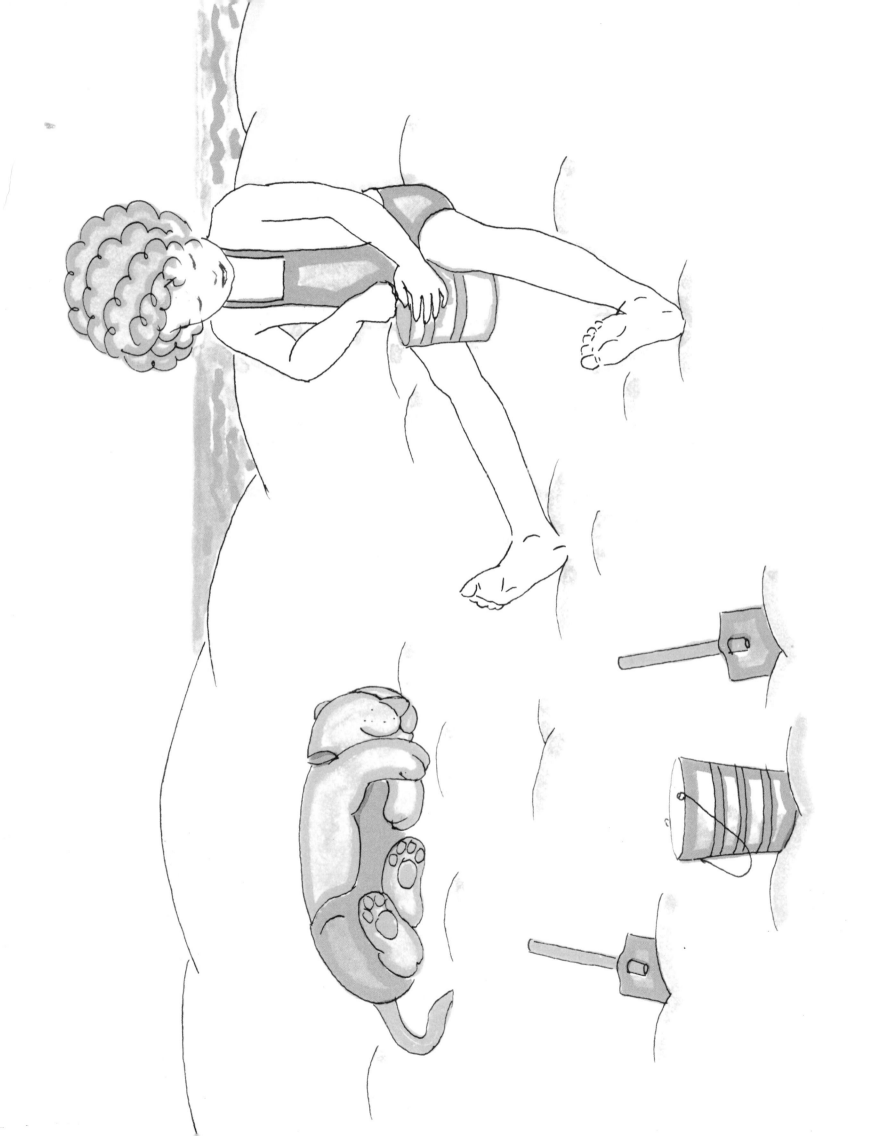

Of course he had sunbaths at the seaside.

And the way he took his codliver oil was simply beautiful.

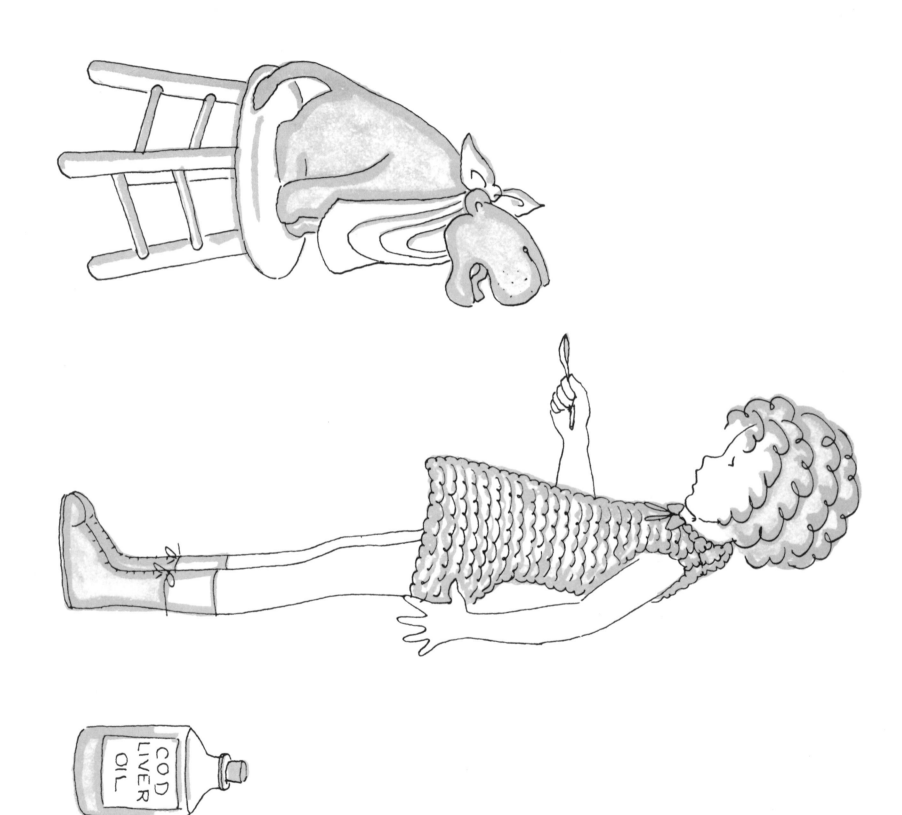

Herbert grew, and *grew*, and GREW!

He was such a friendly lion.

When Sally's grandmother came to the house he always put his paws on her shoulders and licked her face with his big pink tongue.

Sally's grandmother did not really like this but Herbert did it just the same.

He was so friendly.

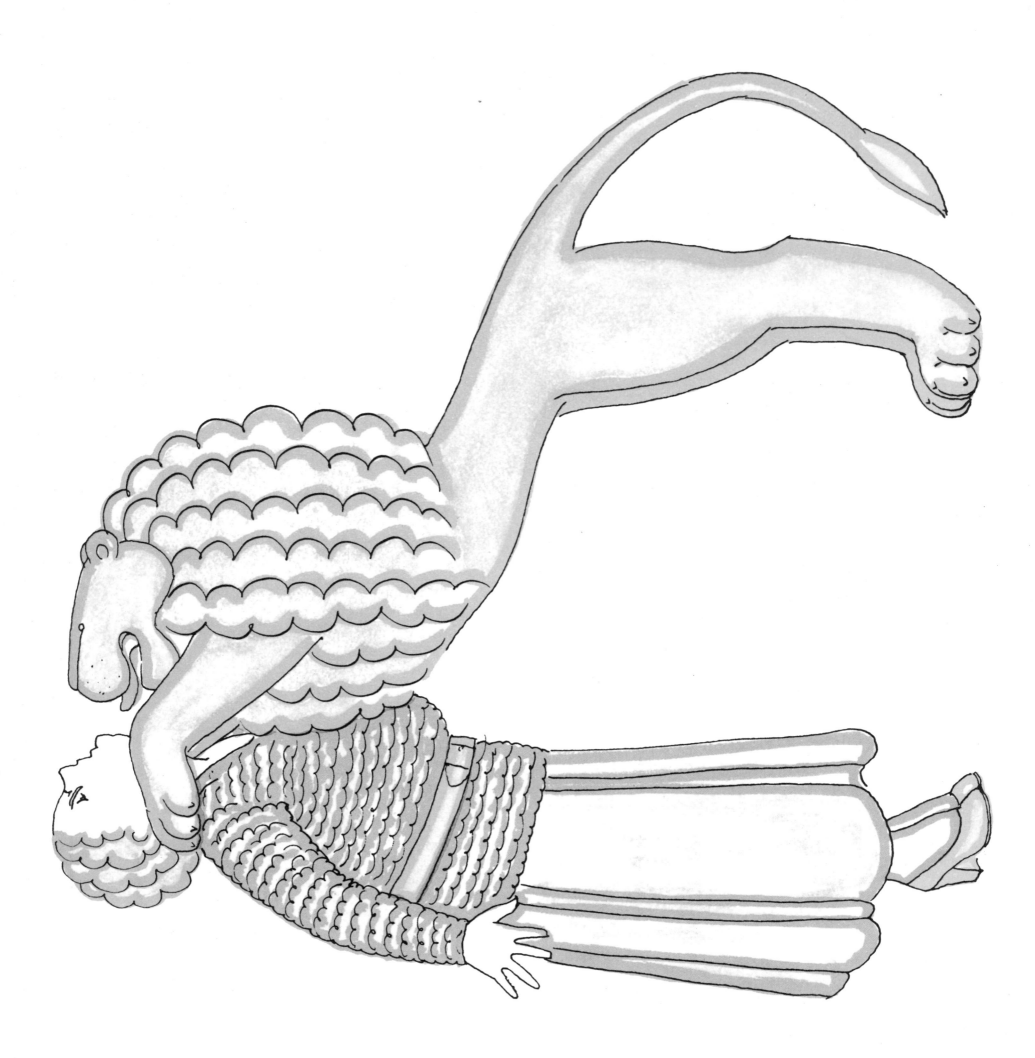

When the milkman or the postman or the grocer

or the butcher's boy came to the door,

Herbert always RAN—

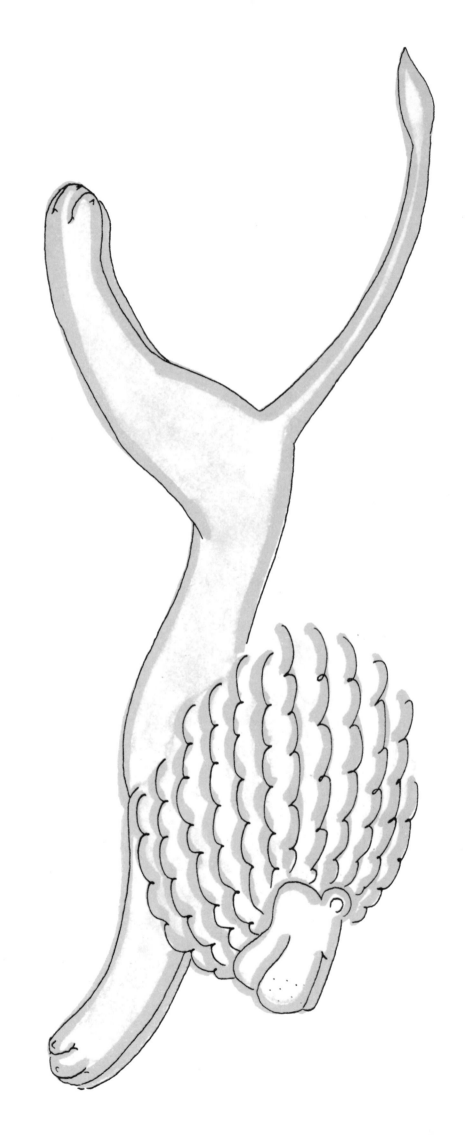

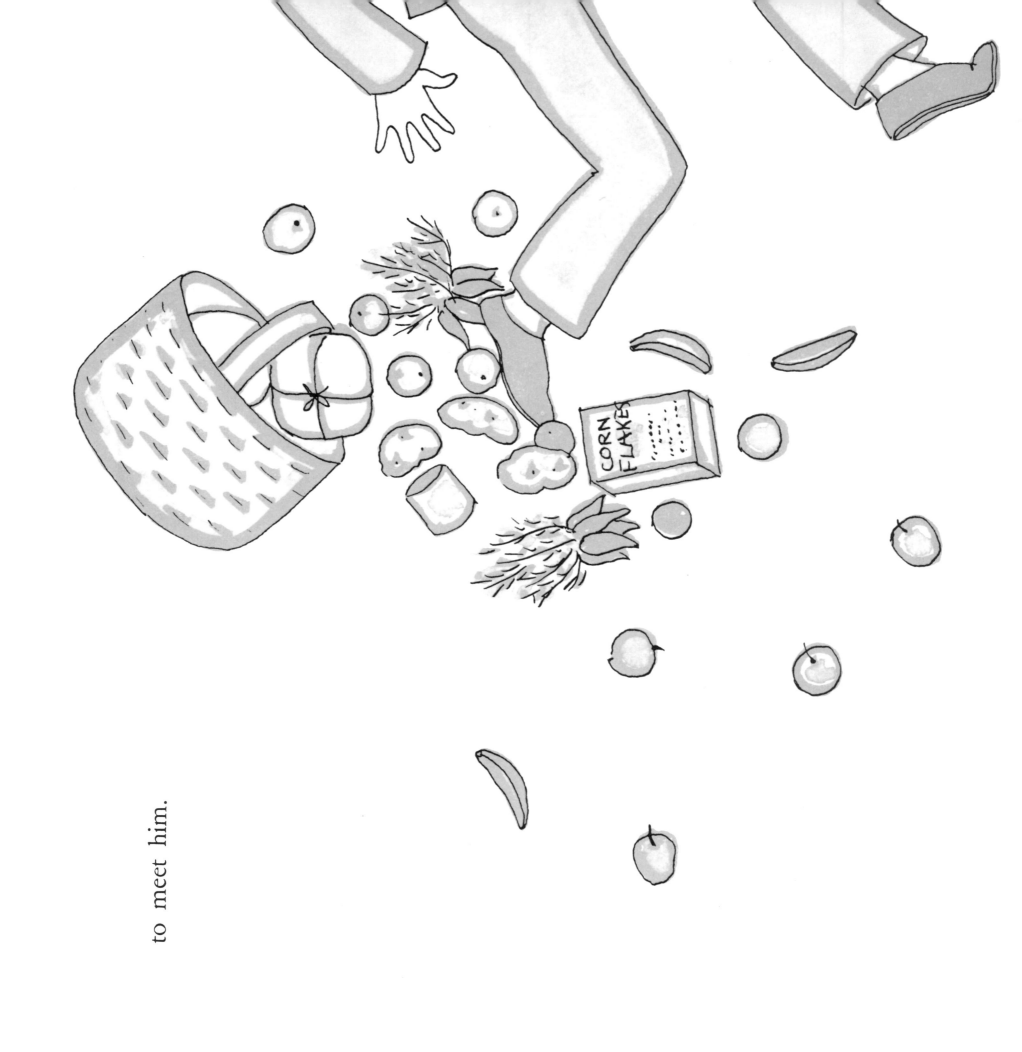

to meet him.

Sally told people over and over that Herbert was just friendly, but they did not believe her.

They were sure he wanted to bite them.

Pretty soon the postman stopped bringing the letters to Sally's house, he was so afraid of poor Herbert.

And the butcher's boy stopped bringing the meat.

And the milkman stopped bringing the milk.

And the grocer stopped bringing the groceries.

And all of Sally's friends stopped coming to see her.

And her grandmother and her grandfather and all her aunts and uncles and cousins stopped coming.

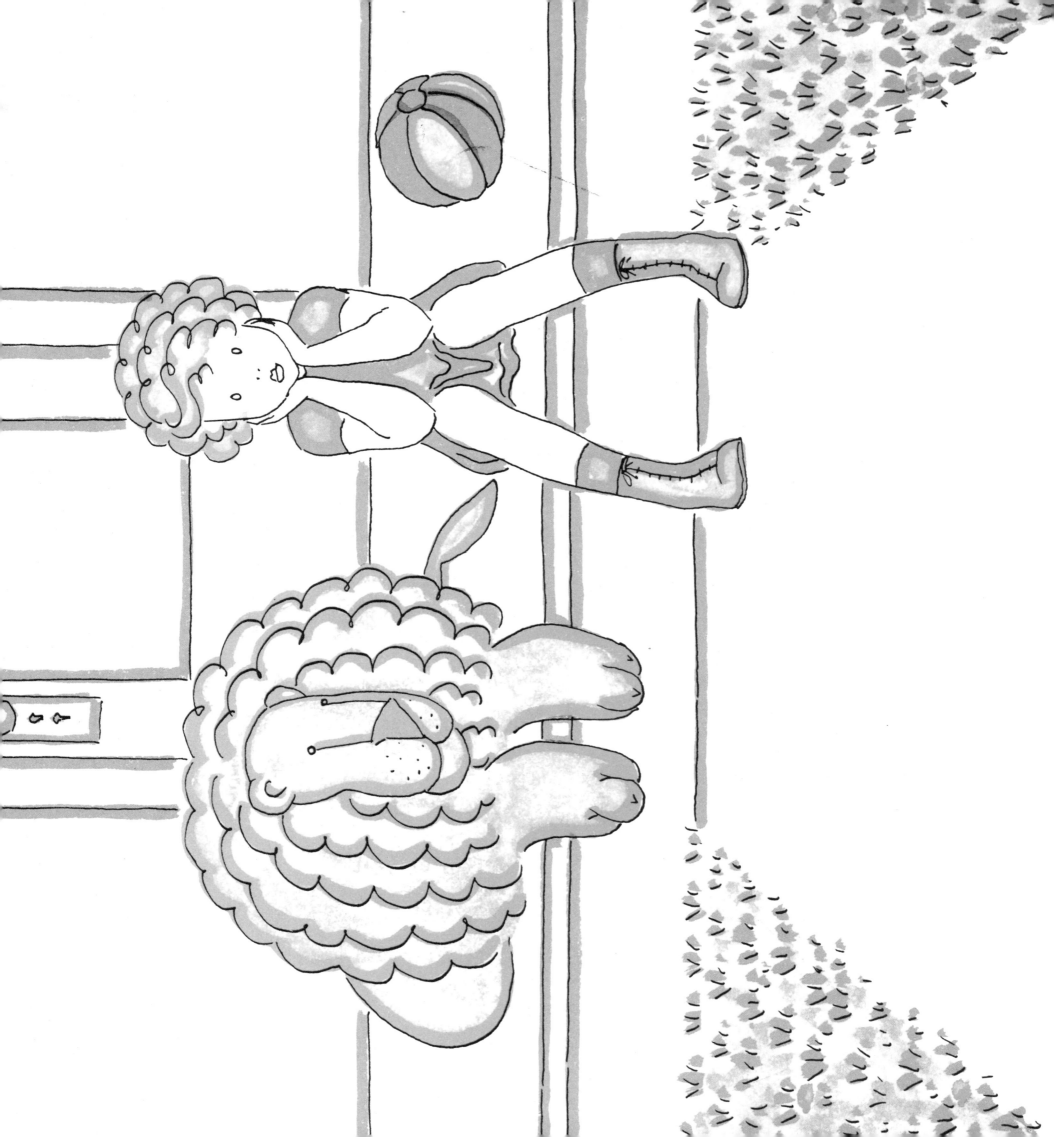

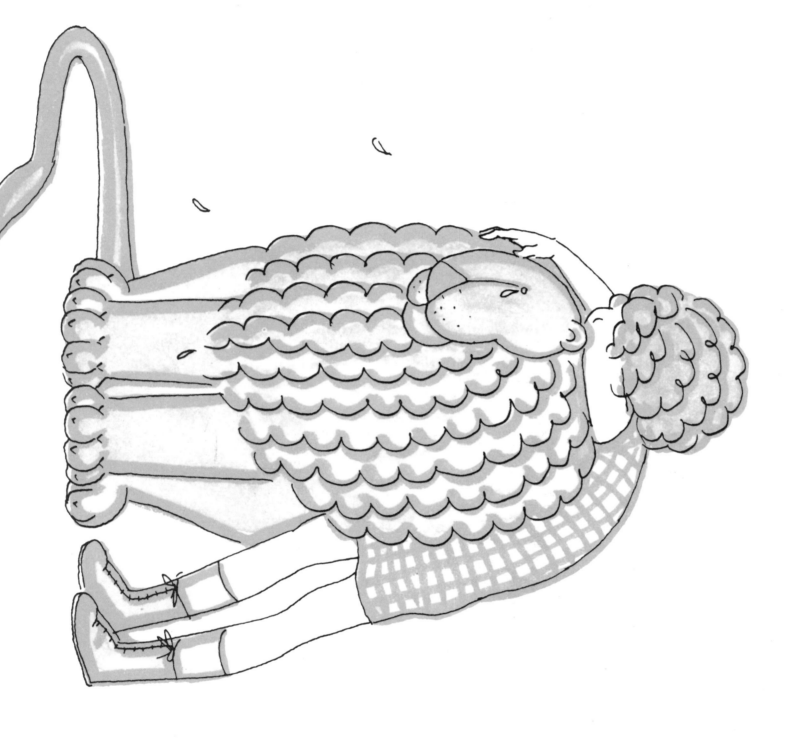

At last Sally's father said Herbert would have to go and live at the Zoo, in a cage with bars, so he could not frighten people any more. Sally cried and cried. And Herbert cried too.

Then Sally's mother had a wonderful idea. "Why not send Herbert to our ranch in the mountains?" she said. "Then he could live outdoors and have plenty of room." So Sally's parents sent Herbert to the mountains. And to keep her from being too lonely without him they gave her a very small kitten.

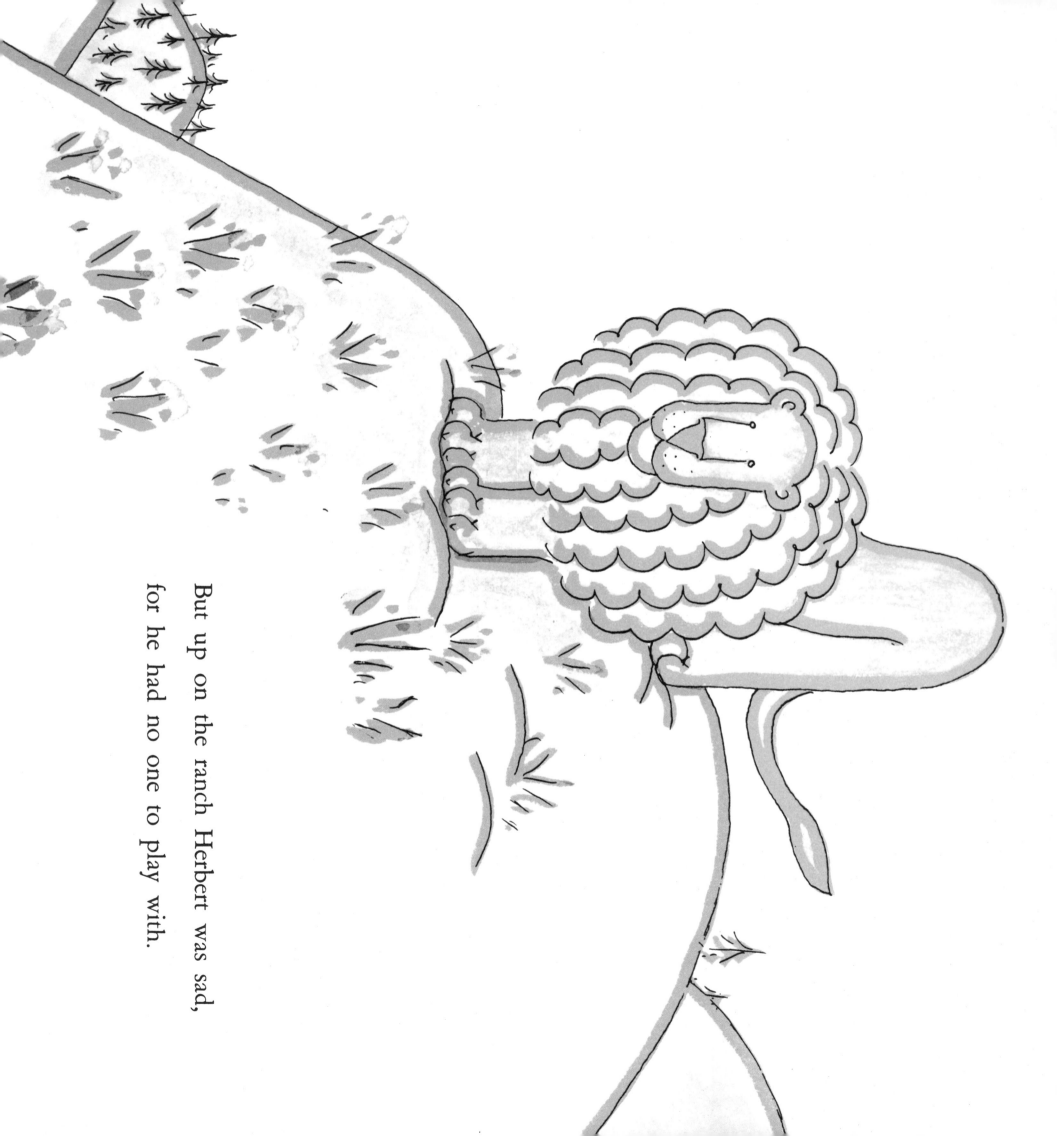

But up on the ranch Herbert was sad,
for he had no one to play with.

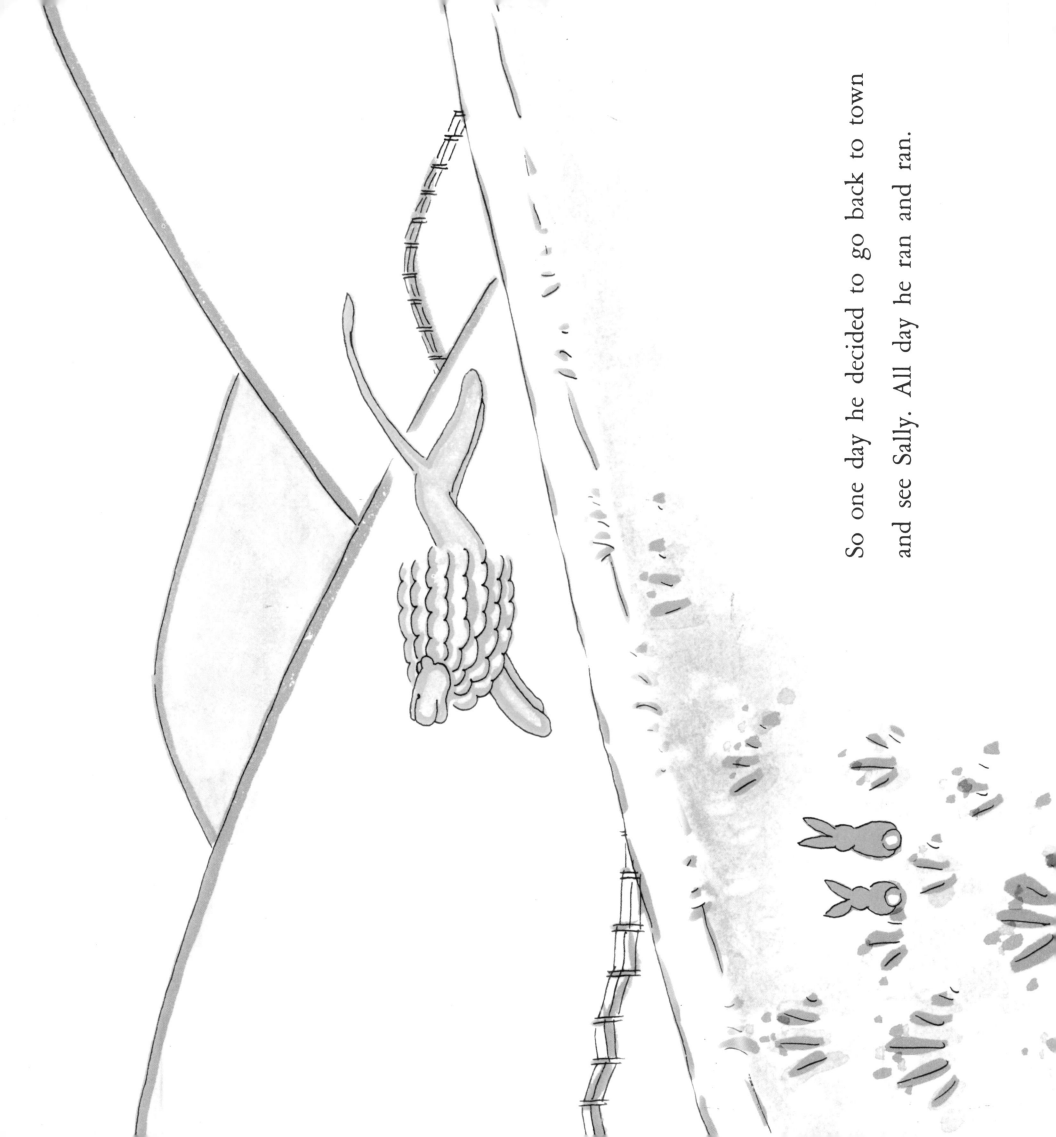

So one day he decided to go back to town and see Sally. All day he ran and ran.

When he got hungry he stopped at places
and ate candy and pie and ice cream cones.
He hadn't any money with him but that was all right,
for no one thought of asking him to pay.

At last he reached Sally's house.
She was delighted to see him.

That night they had an extra-special supper to celebrate, with vanilla ice cream and lemon layer cake.

In the middle of the night Herbert was very ill

with a terrible pain in his stomach.

Nobody knew about all the indigestible things

he had eaten on his way from the ranch,

but even the doctor said Herbert must have eaten *something*.

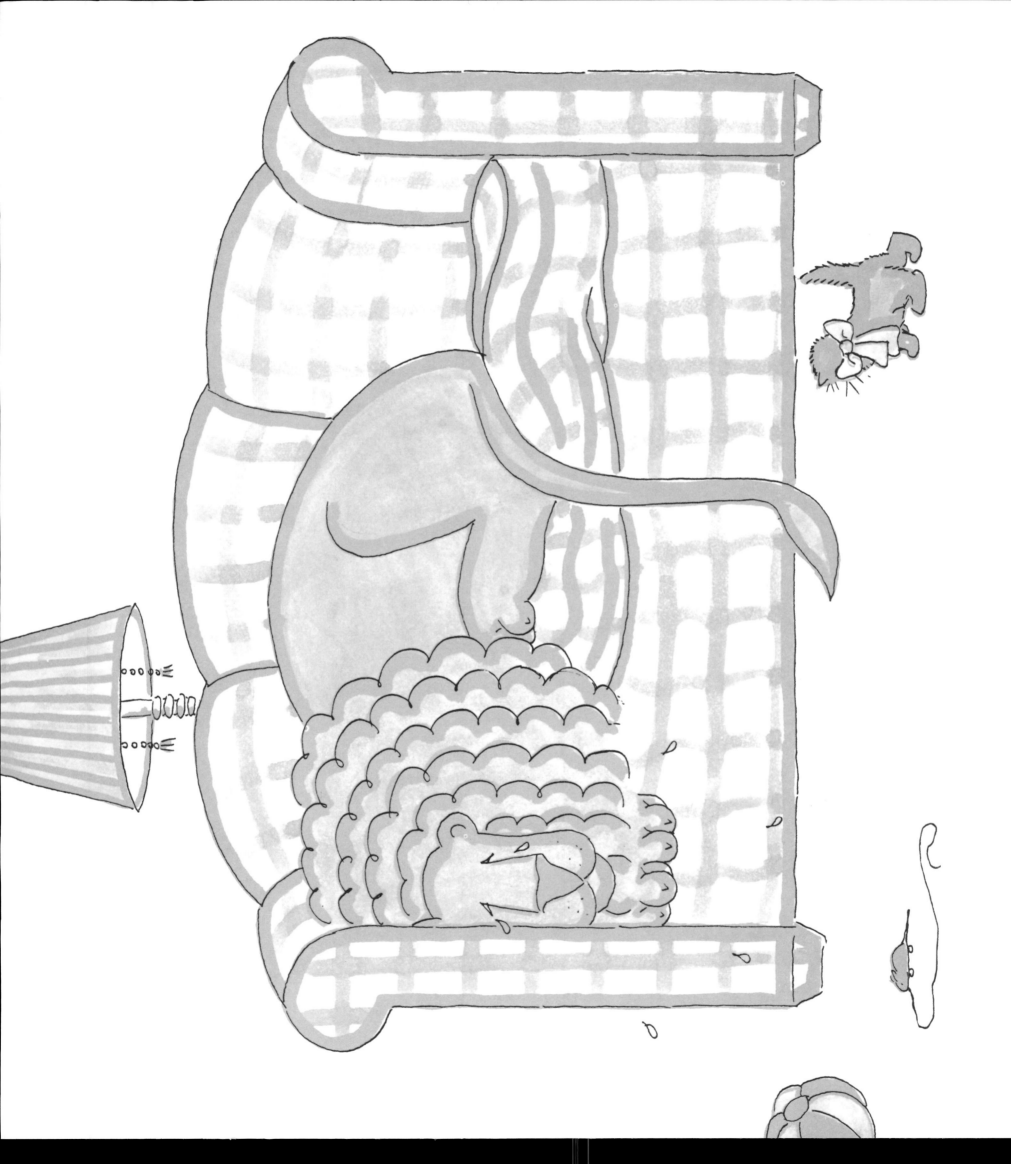

When Herbert was well enough to sit up and eat milk-toast,

Sally's parents had a serious talk about him.

They talked and talked, and finally Sally's father said,

"Well, dear, it looks to me as if the only thing we can do

is move out to the ranch and stay there.

Then Sally and Herbert can play together all the time."

And Sally's mother said, "Darling, I'm afraid you're right.

It's the only thing we can do."

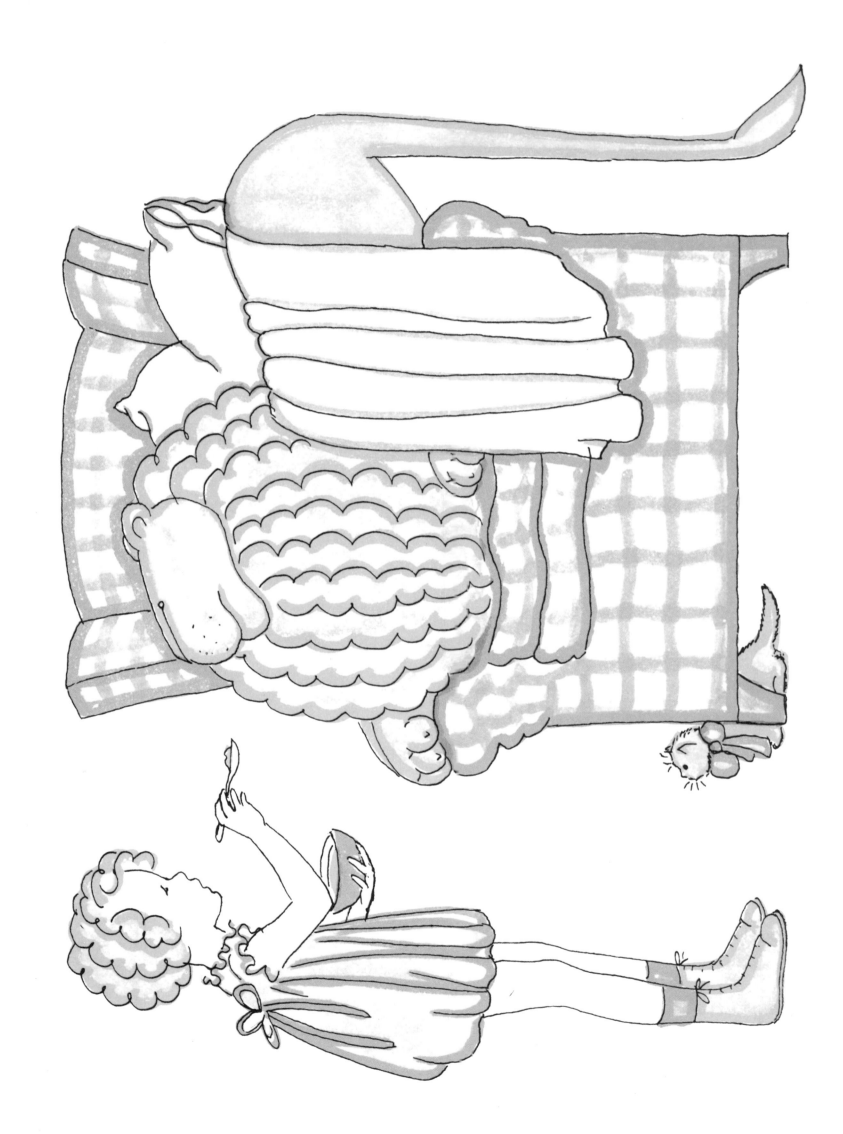

So they packed up everything, and got in the car, and went back to the ranch.

And now Sally's mother and father often say they don't see
how they ever stood it living in the city,
where there isn't any fresh air or scenery,
and the streetcars keep you awake at night.
As for Sally and Herbert, they are *very* happy.
They have each other to play with every day,
and a whole big ranch to play on.
And what more could anyone wish?

THE END

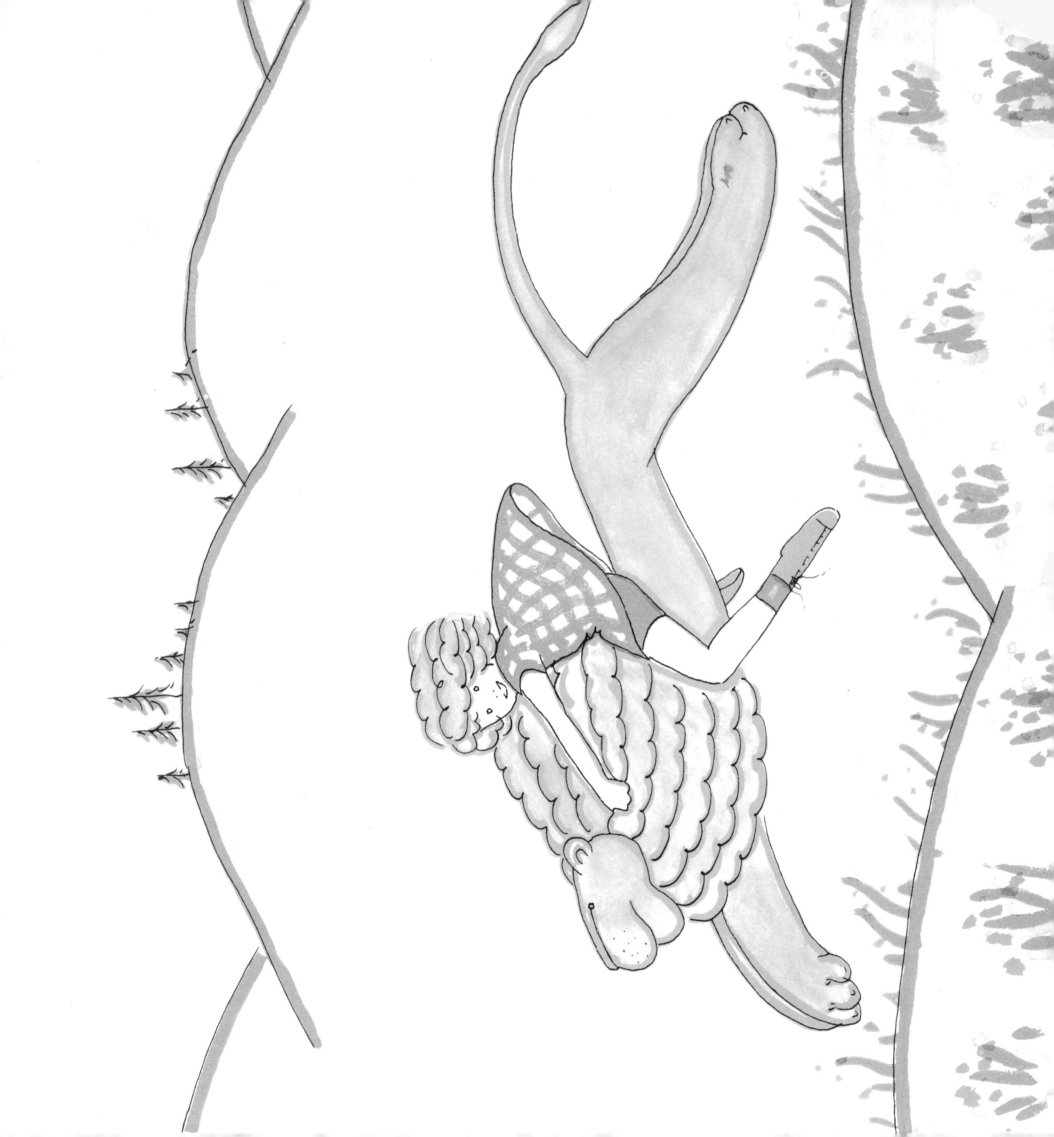

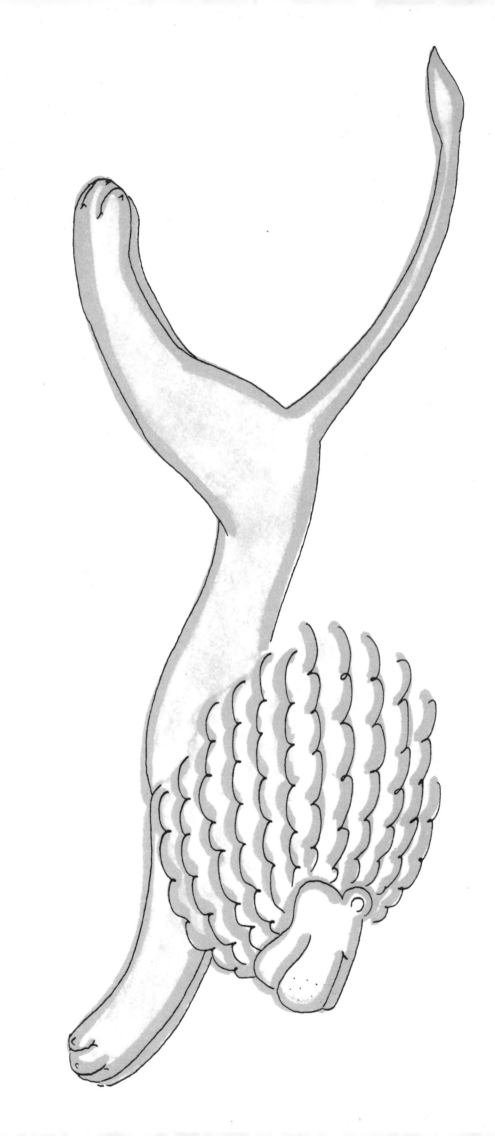